Simple English
to
Smart English

Miss Sarita Singh

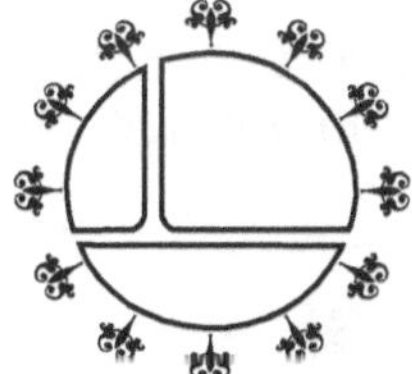

Anjuman Prakashan
Allahabad

ISBN 978-93-86027-93-1

Simple English to Smart English
By : Sarita Singh

Edition: First, 2017

Published By : ANJUMAN PRAKASHAN
942, Mutthiganj, Allahabad, 211003
website - anjumanpublication.com
E-mail : contact@anjumanpublication.com

Distributed by :
www.redgrab.com

Foreward

My association with Sarita has been nearly three years old now. It is a privilege to be in the company of such an enlightened soul. Sarita is not only immensely knowledgeable but is also gem of a person. When I first saw her, she was delivering a lecture on Smart English for which she had specially brought hand written photocopied notes for every student. I was flamboyant to see the amount of hard work that she had done only to enhance the spoken skills of students.

Sarita's interest in Smart English dates back to many years. This book of hers is a result of her endless hard work since the time she was a college student. Sarita has a vast teaching experience of more than twenty years and has taught English and life skills in a myriad of reputed schools across Delhi and NCR. She has been associated with Maharaja Agarsain and Rockwel School ; New Delhi, St. Brijmohan Lal Sr. Sec. School; Faridabad, and is currently teaching in Lucknow Public schools and Colleges; Lucknow.

Emphasising the fact that good command over

English is the need of the hour and is the only assured key to a bright and rewarding career, this book is a pioneering effort to improve the Spoken English of students by using Smart and trendy English . I am sure that the book will make an interesting read and will be enjoyed by students and teachers alike.

With best wishes
MS. Puja Anand
MBA, M.A, M.Phil (English)

From Writer's Pen

Dear Children! I have passed through the same phase of life which now you are undergoing. How I started taking keen interest in English language is an interesting experience. Really dear Children! I want to share it with you.

Those were the days when my father was posted at Shillong as a Scientist. I took admission in Balika Hindi Vidyalaya School in which English was taught from 6th class. After completing my 2nd class I was admitted to 3rd class in kendriya vidayalaya. In 3rd class my English class teacher asked me to read an English lesson, but since I was not well versed in English, She got furious and asked one brilliant boy MC Deepak to slap me for that. MC Deepak came and slapped me forcefully on my cheek. I remember that so vividly and felt as if stars were twinkling before my eyes. There was complete darkness. I put down my head on my desk, but was not crying. I was neither angry with my English teacher nor with MC

Deepak. My anger was on me...repeatedly I was asking myself- 'Why don't I know English?' After that I started hunting for new words to enrich my vocabulary. The words which were long, I used to break them and learn them. This is how I became interested in English and an avid reader. But my basics of this subject became clearer when I started teaching class one, then two, then three and so on. In this way I became a teacher of senior classes. I have taught 9 and 10 classes for seven years. Now I am working as an English teacher of Junior classes in Lucknow Public schools and Colleges.

I have taught all type of students in my life i.e. city students as well as students of village area. My skill to teach Spoken English to a novice came to me when I spent twelve years as an English teacher at St. Brijmohan Lal Sr. Sec. School. This school is situated at Anangpur village, Faridabad, where we used to teach the students through Smart Classes i.e Edu.com. Maximum students of that School were from village background who had no support from their parents in learning i.e most of them were illiterates, but villagers were happy to send their wards to school because we taught them through Digital board. I used to type the English conversation i.e. maximum sentences spoken in class room, playground, market, station, airport etc. It used to take so much time for me to think and also to hunt for new words and sentences from different books, just to teach my students. Though there was no separate period for spoken English, I used to find time in between my course and in arrangement classes to teach them. I used to photocopy those sentences and circulate them amongst my students. I enjoyed teaching there, as I got very good response from students. Even here in Lucknow Public schools and Colleges, I teach Smart English in my arrangement classes which my students appreciate a lot.

This book is the outcome of all those sleepless nights when I used to toil late night for my students. I never crave for appreciation from my Principals. My only reward is when my students who are the building- blocks of our nation are satisfied from my teaching. I have many gems i.e my students who have always been in touch with me. My students mean everything to me.

I thank Puja Ma'am for writing the foreword of this book and also for contributing some Smart English sentences for this book.

Children! I want to tell you that however you reach high in your life, always be down to earth. Eliminate 'I' component from your life, as you see when you prick a needle to a balloon, it bursts. It means a subtle 'Ego' leads to downfall in life. However intelligent we become is the result of what we get from our society, parents, teachers, spiritual masters and elders. Always dedicate your good work to Lord Almighty before sleep. The new idea which comes to your mind is the gift of God, because the God bestows upon you many unique ideas to make HIS wonderful creation more beautiful. Always consider yourself as 'a tool' in HIS hands. Then see the miracles. Don't be full of yourself i.e. never boast yourself.

I thank all the people, friends, teachers, society, reading sources and above all my spiritual master St. Yashpal ji's Spiritual literature and guidance through internal inspiration from where I learnt a lot. May God bless all my children; they are my weapon and they have the calibre to make a New India.

With best wishes.
Miss Sarita Singh

Content

1. Lesson 1 - 11
2. Lesson 2 - 18
3. Lesson 3 - 26
4. Lesson 4 - 34
5. Lesson 5 - 41
6. Lesson 6 - 49
7. Lesson 7 - 57
8. Lesson 8 - 64
9. Lesson 9 - 72
10. Lesson 10 - 80
11. Lesson 11 - 89
12. Lesson 12 - 98
13. Lesson 13 - 106
14. Lesson 14 - 113
15. Lesson 15 - 121
16. Lesson 16 - 129
17. Lesson 16 Words that
    describe people - 136

Simple English to Smart English
Lesson - 1

1. Simple English - Sorry, by mistake I said that.
Smart English - Sorry, It was just a slip of my tongue.

2. Simple English - He is very cunning.
Smart English - He is crafty.

3. Simple English - By mistake I wrote that.
Smart English - It was just a slip of my pen.

4. Simple English - It is his habit.
Smart English - He is accustomed to it.

5. Simple English - His spoken words have spread in the town.
Smart English - His spoken words have become the talk of the town.

6. Simple English - He is my true and faithful friend.

Smart English - He is my bosom friend.

7. Simple English - Come on! Stop it .

Smart English - Come on ! hang it.

8. Simple English - I am unable to understand it clearly.

Smart English - I am bit dazed.

9. Simple English - Pick up the good values from our epics.

Smart English - Cull the good values from our epics.

10. Simple English - Let us sit under the sun and take the warmth of hot sun.

Smart English - Let us bask in the sun.

11. Simple English - Children go on wrong path in bad company.

Smart English - Children go astray in bad company.

12. Simple English - Leave your bad habits.

Smart English - Shun your bad habits.

13. Simple English - Come on! Speak what you want to say.

Smart English - Come on ! speak your mind.

---

14. Simple English - I hope I am not disturbing you.

Smart English - I hope I am not putting you off.

15. Simple English - Daily write down your experiences in your diary.

Smart English - Daily pen down your experiences in your diary.

16. Simple English - If you will tell my secrets then it means you have broken my trust.

Smart English - If you will tell my secrets to anybody then it will be a breach of trust.

17. Simple English - I am having financial problem.

Smart English - I am in financial crunch.

18. Simple English - I don't have money.

Smart English - I am out of my pocket.

19. Simple English - Forget the past .

Smart English - Let bygone be bygone.

20. Simple English - Mummy please serve the food.

Smart English - Mummy please lay the table.

21. Simple English - Get away from my eyes.

Smart English - Buzz off, get away.

22. Simple English - Mummy what is special dish today.

Smart English - Mummy what is the side dish today.

23. Simple English - After all what do you want?

Smart English - What are you up to?

24. Simple English - He does his work at the last moment.

Smart English - He does his work at eleventh hour.

25 Simple English - .He has dropped his idea to compete.

Smart English - The scales have fallen from his eyes.

26. Simple English - He is angry with me.

Smart English - He is cross with me.

27. Simple English - He couldn't make much recovery after accident.

Smart English - He couldn't make much headway after accident.

28. Simple English - He is well paid Zone sales manager.

Smart English - He is hard charging zone manager.

29. Simple English - His application has been rejected.

Smart English - His application has been turned down.

30. Simple English - He solved the problem in few minutes.

Smart English - He worked out the problem in a few minutes.

31. Simple English - He removed his hat.
Smart English - He took off his hat.

32. Simple English - Kuldeep and sunny have quarrelled again.
Smart English - Kuldeep and sunny have fallen out again.

33. Simple English - His new book is selling too much.
Smart English - His new book is selling like a hot cake.

34. Simple English - I can't tolerate this insult.
Smart English - I can't put up with this insult.

35. Simple English - She is easily be fooled by others.
Smart English - She is easily carried away by others.

36. Simple English - They have cancelled the strike.
Smart English - They have called off the strike.

37. Simple English - Don't tell it to anybody.
Smart English - Keep it to yourself.

38. Simple English - This talk I only heard it, don't believe it.
Smart English - It is only hearsay, don't believe it.

39. Simple English - Love gives birth to love and evil gives birth to evil.

Smart English - Love begets love, and evil begets evil.

4o. Simple English - I am unable to do this work. I can't do this.

Smart English - It is not my cup of tea.

41. Simple English - Everybody can't do this work.

Smart English - It is not everybody's ball of court.

42. Simple English - Use your own intelligence.

Smart English - Use your own wits.

43. Simple English - Be the most beautiful flower on the chest of the earth.

Smart English - Be the most beautiful flower on the bosom of the earth.

44. Simple English - My car stopped functioning on the highway.

Smart English - My car broke down on the highway.

45. Simple English - There is evil person in every society.

Smart English - There is a black sheep in every society.

46. Simple English - The Noble Prize is the greatest honour for a scholar.

Smart English - The noble prize is a blue ribbon for a scholar.

47. Simple English - Patel was a person of strong will.

Smart English - Patel was a man of cast iron will.

48. Simple English - Don't be proud of your royal family.

Smart English - Don't be proud of your blue blood.

49. Simple English - My soul is hurt.

Smart English - My soul is lacerated.

50. Simple English - She hurt me emotionally.

Smart English - She tormented me a lot.

Simple English to Smart English

Lesson - 2

1. Simple English - A soldier must not be coward.

Smart English - A soldier must not be chicken hearted.

2. Simple English - She shed her showy tears.

Smart English - She shed crocodile tears.

3. Simple English - Today we find fake family relations.

Smart English - Today we find hollow familial relations.

4. Simple English - A candidate gets credit for good handwriting.

Smart English - A candidate gets credit for fair hand.

5. Simple English - He spends too much money.

Smart English - He is extravagant.

6. Simple English - He is lazy.

Smart English - He is lethargic.

7. Simple English - He remains far from others.

Smart English - He keeps himself aloof from others.

8. Simple English - Holi is an enjoyable day for Hindus.

Smart English - Holi is a gala day for Hindus.

9. Simple English - Public was going crazy for Sharukh Khan.

Smart English - Public was going gaga for Sharukh Khan.

10. Simple English - If you hope to pass, you are a fool to hope for that.

Smart English - If you hope to pass, you are in a fool's paradise.

11. Simple English - The coughing of this old man at the music conference disturbed all.

Smart English - The coughing of this old man at the music conference was a fly in the ointment.

12. Simple English - A person who listens his wife's scolding cannot help his brother.

Smart English - A hen- pecked husband cannot help his brother.

13. Simple English - He was saved with little escape in an

accident.

Smart English - In the accident he had a hair – breadth escape.

14. Simple English - The riot was suppressed strictly.

Smart English - The riot was suppressed with an iron hand.

15.-Simple English - He made fun of me in school meeting.

Smart English - He made me a laughing- stock in school meeting.

16. Simple English - Dr. Jha was a learned man.

Smart English - Dr.Jha was a man of letters.

17. Simple English - Pandit Nehru was an extraordinary man.

Smart English - Pandit Nehru was a man of parts.

18. Simple English - What can you expect from an unfaithful and petty man.

Smart English - What can you expect from a man of straw.

19. Simple English - This bill is still pending without any judgment.

Smart English - This bill is still a moot point.

20. Simple English - Shakespear wrote his plays during

---

his prosperous days.

Smart English - Shakespear wrote his play during his palmy days.

21. Simple English - Several inventions have proved to be a bane in form of boon for mankind.

Smart English - Several inventions have proved to be a pandora's box.*

22. Simple English - This work seems to be never ending.

Smart English - This work seems to be penelope's web.*

23. Simple English - Every nurse gets money for clothes etc.

Smart English - Every nurse gets pin money.

24. Simple English - He refuses clearly to help me.

Smart English - He refuses point blank to help me.

25. Simple English - He is Psycho (mad).

Smart English - He is queer fish.

26. Simple English - 15 th August is an important day in India.

Smart English - 15th August is a red letter day in India.

27. Simple English - Grammar, to some people is a scary thing.

Smart English - Grammar to some people is like a red rag to a bull.

28. Simple English - I cannot depend upon him, because he is not reliable person.

Smart English - I cannot depend upon him because he is a broken reed.

29. Simple English - Men like Mahatma Gandhi are the great personality on this earth.

Smart English - Men like Mahatma Gandhi are the salt of the earth.

30. Simple English - Even a small man like me can do some service to the country.

Smart English - - Even a small fry like me can do some service to the country.

31. Simple English - I am fed up of his misconduct.

Smart Engish - I am sick of his misconduct.

32. Simple English - She is very well at cooking.

Smart English - She is a capital hand at cooking.

33. Simple English - You must help your friend.

Smart English - You must back up your friend.

34. Simple English - When all were silent, I broke the silence.

Smart English - When all were silent, I broke the ice.

35. Simple English - Don't cry over the past.
Smart English - Don't brood over the past.

36. Simple English - Don't defame your family by your bad deeds.
Smart English - Don't cast a slur upon your great family.

37. Simple English - She performed very badly on the stage.
Smart English - She cut a sorry figure on the stage.

38. Simple English - Why do you escape from your teacher's eye?
Smart English - Why do you fight shy of your teacher?

39. Simple English - Boys were asked to make a line.
Smart English - Boys were asked to fall in.

40. Simple English - Keep silence. Hear to me.
Smart English - Please give me your ears.

41. Simple English - The poet expressed his own feelings.
Smart English - The poet gave vent to his own feelings.

42. Simple English - I have renounced the silly customs.
Smart English - I have given the go-by to silly customs.

43. Simple English - Have good relations with your neighbours.

Smart English - Keep in with your neighbours.

44. Simple English - Let us eat in a restaurant.

Smart English - Let us eat out.

45. Simple English - How are your children progressing at school?

Smart English - How are your children getting on at school?

46. Simple English - We have no sugar at home.

Smart English - We've run out of sugar.

47. Simple English - What time shall we start a journey?

Smart English - What time shall we set off for a journey?

48. Simple English - Thank you for wishing me New year. Same to you.

Smart English - Thank you. I reciprocate the same to you.

49. Simple English - Don't make me unhappy.

Smart English - Don't dismay me.

50. Simple English - He is unable to move in fear or surprise.

Smart English - He is transfixed with amazement.

---

*Pandora's Box was a large jar given to Pandora which contained all the evils of the world. Pandora opened the jar and all the evils flew out, leaving only "Hope" inside once she had closed it again.

* Penelope's web means anything which is perpetually doing but never done. An endless job.

Usage- The removal of poverty is penelope's web.

Simple English to Smart English

Lesson - 3

1. Simple English - Very carefully he approached me.

Smart English - He approached me gingerly.

2. Simple English - Neither of you cared to tolerate with me.

Smart English - Neither of you cared to put up with me.

3. Simple English - Close the front door.

Smart English - Fasten the front door or bolt the front door.

4. Simple English - Don't look so silly.

Smart English - Don't look so daft.

5. Simple English - She has secret plan to get benefit.

Smart English - She is very scheming.

6. Simple English - She took rest in her bed room after a hard work of day.

Smart English - She retired to her bed room after a hard work.

7. Simple English - He is working on this idea without seriousness.

Smart English - He is toying with this idea.

8. Simple English - Keep on doing it to achieve success.

Smart English - Don't Stop! Make a go of it.

9. Simple English - It was an easy progress and living for me, for several years.

Smart English - It was a smooth sailing for me for several years.

10. Simple English - Ok. I am going now.

Smart English - Ok. I am off now.

11. Simple English - Same thing is with me.

Smart English - We are sailing in the same boat.

12. Simple English - He speaks very sweetly and politely but she is very cunning. Beware of her.

Smart English - You must beware of her tricks as she has an oily tongue.

13. Simple English - Don't recall old happenings, usually

unpleasant one. Think ahead.

Smart English - You should not think of the future as it is useless to flog the dead horse.

14. Simple English - To get our work done we have to give the bribe to the officials there.

Smart English - To get our work done we have to grease the palms of officials there.

15. Simple English - The day of Diwali is a day of rejoicing for all.

Smart English - The day of Diwali is a gala day for all.

16. Simple English - All people of the town went to listen to the Prime Minister.

Smart English - People of the town went the whole hog to listen to Prime Minister.

17. Simple English - He has shunned his bad company and has become a new person.

Smart English - He has given up bad company and thus turned a new leaf in his life.

18. Simple English - Feel comfortable here.

Smart English - Feel at home here.

19. Simple English - Sudden death of his father was really a great loss.

Smart English - The sudden death of his father was a bolt

from the blue for him.

20. Simple English - He visit this place very rarely.

Smart English - He visit this place only once in a blue moon.

21. Simple English - He visit this place very rarely and after a long intervals.

Smart English - His visits to this place are few and far between.

22. Simple English - He arrived at the station just on time.

Smart English - He arrived at the station in the nick of time.

23. Simple English - I usually study books in very early hours.

Smart English - I usually read books in wee hours.

24. Simple English - He is a complete gentleman.

Smart English - He is a gentleman through and through.

25. Simple English - Such jackets are selling too cheap.

Smart English - Such jackets are selling dirt cheap.

26. Simple English - He seems being too crazy.

Smart English - He seems to be having a bee in his bonnet.

---

27. Simple English - Youth is a short –lived blessing.

Smart English - Youth is a nine days wonder.

28. Simple English - I found him totally engrossed in day dreaming and serious thought.

Smart English - I found him engrossed in a brown study.

29. Simple English - After his father's death he wasted his money.

Smart English - After his father's death he played ducks and drakes with money.

30. Simple English - you do not have a small possibility to pass the examination.

Smart English - You do not have a ghost's chance to pass the examination.

31. Simple English - She is very fond of eating sweet things and can't resist eating chocolates.

Smart English - She has a sweet tooth, and can't resist eating chocolates.

32. Simple English - An average minister is only a yes man of the Prime Minister.

Smart English - An average minister is only a Man Friday of the Prime Minister.

33. Simple English - Let us give up enmity and live like brothers.

Smart English - Let's bury the hatchet and live like brothers.

34. Simple English - The robbers killed the trader.
Smart English - The robbers made away with the trader.

35. Simple English - 'Sati' system was abolished long ago.
Smart English - 'Sati' was done away with long ago.

36. Simple English - He says what he is not.
Smart English - He is double faced.

37. Simple English - It's raining heavily.
Smart English - It's raining cats and dogs

38. Simple English - Bring a glass of water for me.
Smart English - Fetch a glass of water for me.

39. Simple English - Do your own work, don't disturb me.
Smart English - Mind your own business, Don't disturb me.

40. Simple English - I am feeling sleepy.
Smart English - I am feeling drowsy.

41. Simple English - Speak carefully.
Smart English - Mind your tongue.

42. Simple English - The train stops at only important stations.

Smart English - The train calls at only important stations.

43. Simple English - There are many clever men who keep on siding with both the rivals.

Smart English - There are many clever men who run with the hare and hunt with the hunters.

44. Simple English - Politics is being mysterious these days.

Smart English - Politics has become a red herring these days.

45. Simple English - You must listen to your teachers attentively when she is speaking.

Smart English - You must lend your ears to your teachers when she is speaking.

46. Simple English - He doesn't give any heed to my advice.

Smart English - He turned a deaf ear to my advice.

47. Simple English - You may argue against my view point but I am firm on it.

Smart English - You may argue against my view point, but I stick to my guns.

48. Simple English - Children shouted loudly when they saw the robbers.

Smart English - Children raised a hue and cry when they saw the robbers.

49. Simple English - India's dream to be a developed nation is still in process of forming.

Smart English - India's dream to be a developed nation is still in pipeline.

50. Simple English - Some officers are in the habit of accepting bribe.

Smart English - Some officers are in the habit of accepting hush money.

Simple English to Smart English

Lesson - 4

1. Simple English - It is a total lie to say that India has no past culture.

Smart English - It is a white lie to say that India has no past culture.

2. Simple English - He is very unpleasant person.

Smart English - He is shitty person.

3. Simple English - His hard labour was futile.

Smart English - His hard labour was of no avail.

4. Simple English - I was listening him carefully.

Smart English - I was all ears to his speech.

5. Simple English - I have a helper who always does what I want.

Smart English - I have a helper at my back & call.

6. Simple English - He was quite good in mathematics.

Smart English - He was quite at home in mathematics.

7. Simple English - Nehru was born in a rich family.

Smart English - Nehru was born with a silver spoon in his mouth.

8. Simple English - I am not of same opinion with you.

Smart English - I am not at one with you.

9. Simple English - Books are lying here and there.

Smart English - Books are lying at sixes and sevens.

10. Simple English - When he failed, he didn't know what to do.

Smart English - When he failed, he was at his wit's end.

11. Simple English - When monsoon fails, farmers look very sad and disappointed.

Simple English - When monsoon fails farmers look as though they were in the doldrums.

12. Simple English - The boy was very afraid when his pen broke in the examination.

Smart English - The boy was in fix when his pen broke in the examination.

---

13. Simple English - He follows what he preaches in his speech.

Smart English - His action is in keeping with his speech.

14. Simple English - Who is in this chair at this meeting?

Smart English - Meeting is presided by whom?

15. Simple English - A good boy / girl is liked by the teacher.

Smart English - A good / girl is in the good books of his / her teacher.

16. Simple English - Vinoba Ji is always on top of the other thinkers.

Smart English - Vinoba Ji is always in the van of thinkers.

17. Simple English - My spiritual Master St. Yashpal ji is number one.

Smart English - My spiritual master St. Yashpal ji is numero uno.

18. Simple English - Capitalism is now going down day by day.

Smart English - Capitalism is on the wan now.

19. Simple English - Colonialism is now at its last.

Smart English - Colonialism is on its last legs.

20. Simple English - He was absent because he was not

feeling well today.

Smart English - He was absent because he was out of sorts today.

21. Simple English - I do not care if you go against me because your opposition is useless.

Smart English - I don't care if you go against me because your opposition is neither here nor there.

22. Simple English - He is very proud.

Smart English - He is full of himself.

23. Simple English - He helped me in the beginning but afterwards he didn't.

Smart English - He helped me in the beginning but backed out at last.

24. Simple English - You must help your friend.

Smart English - You must back up your friend.

25. Simple English - Our enemy had to be insulted in the last war of Kargil.

Smart English - Our enemy had to bite the dust in the last war of Kargil.

26. Simple English - The farmer is starting the work / plan.

Smart English - The farmer is breaking ground.

---

27. Simple English - I told him about his father's death.

Smart English - I broke the news to him about his father's death.

28. Simple English - I saw the thief but he ran away.

Smart English - I saw thief but he broke away.

29. Simple English - Sending armed forces to control these children is like using so big power to small work.

Smart English - Sending armed forces to control these children is like breaking a fly on the wheel.

30. Simple English- My brother scolded me.

Smart English- My brother rebuked me.

31. Simple English - Riya outburst in anger and destroyed her magic mirror.

Smart English - In a tantrum, Riya destroyed her magic mirror.

32. Simple English - A seminar on teaching method was held.

Smart English - A seminar on pedagogy was held.

33. Simple English - It is the duty and responsibility of teachers to make children a good citizen.

Smart English - It is the onus of teachers to make children a good citizen.

34. Simple English - I have firm faith on God.

Smart English - I have unflinching faith on God.

35. Simple English - She is pure by heart.

Smart English - She is pious by heart.

36. Simple English - You are too worried about future.

Smart English - You are too apprehensive about future.

37. Simple English - She is not bound by anything.

Smart English - She is unfettered by anything.

38. Simple English - My mother is busy in day today work.

Smart English - My mother is busy in daily chores.

39. Simple English - He trains his horse every morning.

Smart English - He breaks in horse every morning.

40. Simple English - A thief entered into my house.

Smart English - A thief broke into my house.

41. Simple English - Dengu has spread in the town.

Smart English - Dengu has broken out in the town.

42. Simple English - The college is closed for holidays.

Smart English - The college broke up for holidays.

43. Simple English - Trees bear new leaves in spring.

Smart English - Trees bring forth new leaves in spring.

44. Simple English - India & Pakistan are now trying to solve their differences or enmity

Smart English - India and Pakistan are now trying to bury the hatchet.

45. Simple English - My friend came at my home.

Smart English - My friend called at my home.

46. Simple English - He was bold enough to speak clearly.

Smart English - He was bold enough to call a spade a spade.

47. Simple English - The cry took my attention.

Smart English - The cry called off my attention.

48. Simple English - I cannot remember that old incident.

Smart English - I cannot call up that old incident.

49. Simple English - He worked according to my wishes.

Smart English - He carried out my wishes.

50. Simple English - Our college team won the match.

Smart English - Our college team carried the day in the match.

Simple English to Smart English

Lesson - 5

1. Simple English - The SP solved the matters sternly.

Smart English - The SP carried the matter with a high hand.

2. Simple English - My book was much more superior to others.

Smart English - My book cast all others into the shade.

3. Simple English - The secret is now open .

Smart English - The secret has now come to light.

4. Simple English - How did the accident happen?

Smart English - How did the accident came to pass?

5. Simple English - His result was not as per my expectation.

Smart English - His result came short of my expectation.

6. Simple English - At the M.A examination my brother passed with good marks.

Smart English - At the M.A examination my brother came off with flying colours.

7. Simple English - I rely on my friends vote.

Smart English - I count upon my friends vote.

8. Simple English - Make your speech short.

Smart English - Cut short your speech.

9. Simple English - His misbehavior hurt me.

Smart English - His misbehavior cut me to the quick.

10. Simple English - India alone can solve the difficult problems in an extraordinary way of world peace.

Smart English - India alone can cut the Gordian knot of world peace.

11. Simple English - His speech had no impact on people.

Smart English - His speech cut no ice on people.

12. Simple English - You should behave properly with your helper.

Smart English - You should deal well to your helper.

13. Simple English - What does your argument aim at?

Smart English - What does your argument drive at?

14. Simple English - He lives in a dirty house.

Smart English - He resides/ dwells in a dirty house.

15. Simple English - He encouraged him to murder.

Smart English - He egged him to murder.

16. Simple English - The officer had to face the scolding for his negligence.

Smart English - The officer had to face the music for his negligence.

17. Simple English - She is grinning at me like a foolish person.

Smart English - She is grinning at me like a simpleton.

18. Simple English - It is not proper to go against one's master.

Smart English - It is not proper to fall foul of one's master.

19. Simple English - He is a city boy.

Smart English - He is a city-bred.

20. Simple English - Sometimes even best friends fight.

Smart English - Sometimes even best friends fall out.

---

21. Simple English - Old laws are not being followed.

Smart English - Old laws are falling into obeyance.

22. Simple English - He is victim of cholera.

Smart English - He fall prey to cholera.

23. Simple English - My resolution became futile for want of support.

Smart English - My resolution fell to ground for want of support.

24. Simple English - You must have something for support in old age.

Smart English - You must have something to fall back upon in old age.

25. Simple English - All my appeals had no impact on the mob.

Smart English - All my appeal fall flat on the mob.

26. Simple English - I have to bear the expenses of the party.

Smart English - I have to foot the bill of the party.

27. Simple English - Smugglers tried to take the advantage of the circumstances.

Smart English - Smugglers tried to fish in troubled waters during the war.

28. Simple English - I overcame the difficulty at last.

Smart English - I got over the difficulty at last.

29. Simple English - He was in trouble for committing a theft.

Smart English - He got into hot water for committing a theft.

30 . Simple English - The car horn is annoying me.

Smart English - The car horn is getting on my nerves.

31. Simple English - That music is irritating me.

Smart English - That music is starting to get on my nerves.

32. Simple English - Will you stop doing that? I am getting irritated.

Smart English - Will you stop doing that? It is getting on my nerves.

33. Simple English - He is an important / powerful person.

Smart English - He is a big cheese.

34. Simple English - This story is not true. It is unbelievable.

Smart English - It is a cock and bull story.

35. Simple English - I was trying to talk to Rohit, but my sister kept interrupting.

Smart English - I was trying to talk to Rohit, but my sister kept cutting in.

36. Simple English - I was so tired that I slept well.

Smart English - I was so tired that I slept like a log all night.

 Or

 I slept like a baby.

37. Simple English - Don't encourage him to fight.

Smart English - Don't egg him on to fight.

38. Simple English - I ate my breakfast quickly.

Smart English - I wolfed down my breakfast.

39. Simple English - When I try to ask my boss for a raise, he ignores .

Smart English - When I try to ask my boss for a raise,he brushes me off.

40. Simple English - If you make a mistake, just erase it and start again.

Smart English - If you make a mistake, just erase and start over.

41. Simple English - Be realistic.

Smart English - Keep your feet on the ground.

42. Simple English - Rita wanted me to get her a job. She was pursuing the wrong person.

Smart English - Rita wanted me to get her a job. She was barking up the wrong tree.

43. Simple English - Yuvi is very detail – oriented, but he is not able to see a situation from a broder perspective .

Smart English - Yuvi is very detail- oriented, but not able to see the forest for tree.

44. Simple English - Meeta thought it would be great to go to private school, things always look better on other side.

Smart English - Meeta thought it would be great to go to private school, Grass always look greener on the other side.

45. Simple English - Mamta grows green plants with little efforts.

Smart English - Mamta has a green thumb.

46. Simple English - Really this problem is difficult to deal with.

Smart English - Really this problem is difficult . It is a hot potato.

47. Simple English - We started our journey early the next morning.

Smart English - We set off early the next morning.

48. Simple English - Our TV set doesn't shows the picture

well. It is not working right.

Smart English - Our TV set doesn't shows the picture well it is not working right. It is on the blink.

49. Simple English - He stopped eating sugary sweets.

Smart English - He cut back on sugary sweets.

50. Simple English - I was ill with flue yesterday.

Smart English - I came down with the flue yesterday.

Simple English to Smart English

Lesson -6

1. Simple English - We heard a rumour about the proposed taxation beforehand.

SmartEnglish - We got wind of proposed taxation beforehand.

2. Simple English - When the boy came late again, I scolded him.

Smart English - When the boy came late again, I gave him a bit of my mind.

3. Simple English - Don't give less importance to your friend.

Smart English - Don't give cold shoulder to your friend.

4. Simple English - We should be away from bad company.

Smart English - We should give a wide berth to bad

company.

5. Simple English - Don't give much importance to baseless rumours.

Smart English - Don't give currency to baseless rumours.

6. Simple English - A poet expresses his own feelings.

Smart English - A poet gives vent to his own feelings.

7. Simple English - I have shunned silly customs.

Smart English - I have done go – bye to silly customs.

8. Simple English - If I keep on with my work, I will do it.

Smart English - If I go on with my work, I will do it.

9. Simple English - You have no business to interrupt in our conversation.

Smart English - You have no business to chop in our conversation.

10. Simple English - You must carry out my orders quickly.

Smart English - You must carry my orders chop- chop.

11. Simple English - Having failed in all his attempts,he decided to give up.

Smart English - Having failed in all his attempts, at last he decided to chuck up.

12. Simple English - The old lady was mad with excitement when she saw her son return after many years .

Smart English - The old lady was off her chump when she saw her son return home after many years.

13. Simple English - The Bully's sudden departure from the town was complete riddance for us.

Smart English - The Bully's sudden departure from the town was a clean sweep for us.

14. Simple English - You must confess everything on this matter.

Smart English - You must come clean on this matter.

15. Simple English - There is no doubt that he is completely mad.

Smart English - There is no doubt that he is clean mad.

16. Simple English - By whom the mystery was solved up at last.

Smart English - By whom was the mystery cleared up at last.

17. Simple English - To make himself successful, aim is most important.

Smart English - To make himself successful is the be-all and end- all of his life.

18. Simple English - All his efforts to become a successful actor was futile.

Smart English - All his efforts to become a successful actor ended in smoke.

 Or

All his efforts to become a successful actor ended in fiasco.

19. Simple English - After his defeat the course of his life completely changed.

Smart English - After his defeat he has turned over a new leaf in life.

20. Simple English - He is a person who doesn't stay at one place. He keeps on moving from one country to another.

Smart English - He is a bird of passage and moves from one country to another.

21. Simple English - Money is not easily available.

Smart English - Money doesn't grow on tree.

22. Simple English - People judge your character by what you do.

Smart English - A tree is known by its fruit.

23. Simple English - I want to pass the examination any how.

Smart English - I want to pass the examination by hook or by crook.

24. Simple English - Everything in the room was neat and clean.

Smart English - Everything in the room was spick and span.

25. Simple English - He invited his relatives to the feast.

Smart English - He invited his kith and kin to the feast.

26. Simple English - Every helper is an important part of my family.

Smart English - Every helper is part and parcel of my family.

27. Simple English - This ball is the cause of fight between the two friend.

Smart English - This ball is the apple of discord between two friends.

28. Simple English - Our institute is progressing fast.

Smart English - Our institute is progressing by leaps and bounds.

29. Simple English - The fair was at its peak.

Smart English - The fair was in full swing.

30. Simple English - I am not well today.
Smart English - I am out of sort today.

31. Simple English - Small drop of rain are falling outside.

Smart English - It is drizzling outside.

32. Simple English - Whole night I was changing my side.
Smart English - I kept tossing the whole night.

33. Simple English - He doesn't feel hungry.
Smart English - He feels no appetite.

34. Simple English - His fever is down.
Smart English - His fever has abated.

35. Simple English - He took five rupees from me by false means.
Smart English - He tricked me of five rupees.

36. Simple English - He is spending a lot of time and energy to make a report but result is in vain.
Smart English - He has been chasing his tail all week but the report is still not ready.

37. Simple English - It was really difficult to find the information in spite of trying all the clever means.
Smart English - It was really difficult to find the information even after applying the whole bag of tricks.

38. Simple English - The boss examined my report carefully before submitting to management.
Smart English - The boss examined my report with a fine tooth comb before submitting to management.

39. Simple English - We must try out every possibility to get a result.

Smart English - We must explore all avenues to get a result.

40. Simple English - Before doing something we must get our things well organized.

Smart English - Before doing something we must get our ducks in a row.

41. Simple English - We must be aware of the most recent developments.

Smart English - We must keep our fingers on the pulse about the most recent developments.

42. Simple English - We must know the clever and expert way of doing something.

Smart English - We must know all tricks of the trade to do something.

43. Simple English - He was the first man to lose the job.

Smart English - He was the first man to get the axe.

44. Simple English - It is a well paid job.

Smart English - It is a plum job.

45. Simple English - Two of his juniors are waiting for an opportunity.

Smart English - Two of his juniors are waiting the wings

to get a job.

46. Simple English - He did his best to bring peace and unity.

Smart English - He left no stone unturned to bring peace and unity.

47. Simple English - somehow middle class people fulfill their basic needs.

Smart English - Middle class people live generally from hand to mouth.

48. Simple English - Don't treat people as they treat you.

Smart English - You should not pay the people in the same coin.

49. Simple English - All round development of students is important.

Smart English - Holistic development of students is important.

50. Simple English - Students performed their skills and talents on the stage.

Smart English - Students showcased their skills and talents on the stage.

Simple English to Smart English

Lesson -7

1. Simple English - Students performed a skit on the stage.

Smart English - Students staged a skit.

2. Simple English - Students were given awards on their brilliant performance.

Smart English - Students were felicitated on their brilliant performance.

3. Simple English - A gardener cares the plant.

Smart English - A gardener nurtures the plant.

4. Simple English - It is important to make students aware about environment.

Smart English - It is important to sensitize the students about environment.

5. Simple English - I desire to get good marks.

Smart English - I am desirous to get god marks.

6. Simple English - It is very important to sharpen the skills and talent of the students.

Smart English - It is important to hone the skills and talents of the students.

7. Simple English - Life is full of so many colours.

Smart English - Life is full of so many hues.

8. Simple English - It is sad to see the bad condition of slum children.

Smart English - It is sad to see the plight of children.

9. Simple English - Performance of children won the public.

Smart English - Performance of children enthralled the public.

10. Simple English - Performance of children won the heart of public .

Smart English - Performance of children mesmerized the public.

11. Simple English - Public was amazed to see the performance of students.

Smart English - Public was spell – bound to see the performance of the students.

or

Public was awestruck to see the performance of the students.

12. Simple English - I have realised the danger of dedicating oneself for the cause of public.

Smart English - I have realised the perils of dedicating oneself for the cause of public.

13. Simple English - I am too happy.

Smart English - I am so happy as if I am walking on the moon.

14. Simple English - My heart is jumping with joy.

Smart English - My heart is leaping with joy.

15. Simple English - My joy has no limit.

Smart English - My joy knew no bounds.

16. Simple English - Don't show your anger on me.

Smart English - Don't fire on me.

17. Simple English - She is very pure.

Smart English - She is very pious.

18 Simple English - The boys were doing low job.

Smart English - The boys were doing menial job.

19. Simple English - Work hard and rise up in the sky.
Smart English - Work hard and soar up in the sky.

20. Simple English - Birds are flying in the sky.
Smart English - Birds are soaring in the sky.

21. Simple English - I am desirous for a new job.
Smart English - I am hankering for a new job.

22. Simple English - He doesn't smoke and drink.
Smart English - He is teetotaller.

23. Simple English - His income is low.
Smart English - His income is meagre.

24. Simple English - She did not give any attention to my request.
Smart English - She did not give any heed to my request.

25. Simple English - You have let down my image.
Smart English - You have tarnished my image.

26. Simple English - My eyes were filled up with tears.
Smart English - My eyes were welled up.

27. Simple English - My eyes were filled up with tears.
Smart English - My eyes were brimmed with tears.

28. Simple English - He is too simple.
Smart English - he is naive.

29. Simple English - He is new in service .
Smart English - He is a novice in service.

30. Simple English - Teachers makes the life easy for children.
Smart English - Teachers are facilitators.

31. Simple English - He forgets everything.
Smart English - He is oblivious.

32. Simple English - He is open hearted.
Smart English - He is benign.

33. Simple English - My father forgives all.
Smart English - My father is quite remissive.

34. Simple English - He is too dominating by nature.
Smart English - He is bossy by nature.

35. Simple English - He is very transparent in his work .
Smart English - He is accountable.

36. Simple English - He is moody and enjoys his life.
Smart English - He is whimsical.

---

37. Simple English - My father loves humanity.
Smart English - My father is a true philanthropist.

38. Simple English - His personality attracts others .
Smart English - His personality is charismatic.

39. Simple English - He is very harsh .
Smart English - He is very callous.

40. Simple English - My sister is very friendly.
Smart English - My sister is gregarious.

41. Simple English - She works without thinking.
Smart English - She is impulsive.

42. Simple English - He is bad tempered.
Smart English - He is grumpy.

43. Simple English - Nobody likes my friend.
Smart English - My friend is nasty.

44. Simple English - His behavior is too good.
Smart English - He is affable.

45. Simple English - He is very cheerful.
Smart English - He is convivial .

46. Simple English - She is very straight forward.
Smart English - She is candid.

47. Simple English - She is obedient.
Smart English - She is submissive.

48 . Simple English - My sister responds quickly.
Smart English - My sister is quick – witted.

49. Simple English - My friend is multi talented.
Smart English - My friend is versatile.

50. Simple English - She is not affected by any allegations.
Smart English - She is thick – skinned.

Simple English to Smart English
Lesson -8

1. Simple English - It is very strange.
Smart English - It is weird or It is freaky.

2. Simple English - He is coward.
Smart English - He is funky.

3. Simple English - He has beaten his own record.
Smart English - He bettered his own record.

4. Simple English - It is socially forbidden.
Smart English - It is social taboo.

5. Simple English - Listen some cheerful music.
Smart English - Listen some peppy music.

6. Simple English - Talk to your close friends.
Smart English - Talk to your close buddies.

7. Simple English - It made me work more hard.
Smart English - It made me work doubly hard.

8. Simple English - It was a rude push.
Smart English - It was a rude jolt.

9. Simple English - They didn't stop us.
Smart English - They didn't deter us.

10. Simple English - The programme was celebrated with full zeal and dedication.
Smart English - The programme was celebrated with full fervour and fidelity.

11. Simple English - The activities gave an opportunity to students to be on the stage and emanated LPS confidence.
Smart English - The programme gave an opportunity to the students to be on the stage and exude LPS confidence.

12. Simple English - It was a good decision.
Smart English - It was a judicious decision.

13. Simple English - He is quite fearless.
Smart English - He is dauntless.

---

14. Simple English - Many soldiers showed their unbeaten courage.

Smart English - Many soldiers showed their indomitable courage.

15. Simple English - Vegetable seller was selling vegetables on a trolley.

Smart English - Vegetable seller was selling vegetables on the wheelbarrow.

16. Simple English - He loves the poor.

Smart English - He woos the poor.

17. Simple English - Think over this issue.

Smart English - Mull over this issue.

18. Simple English - Think over this issue.

Smart English - Ponder over this issue.

19. Simple English - Dirty streets and lack of civic sense are hindrance for development.

Smart English - Dirty streets and lack of civic sense are few roadblocks for development.

20. Simple English - They enjoyed their vacation without any problems.

Smart English - They enjoyed their vacation without any hassles.

21. Simple English - Tourist still face heart ranching time while travelling.

Smart English - Tourist still face harrowing time while travelling.

22. Simple English - Our heritage are in ruin.

Smart English - Our heritage are in shambles.

23. Simple English - Film star escape from fans craziness.

Smart English - Film stars escape fan frenzy .

24. Simple English - It is his extreme patriotism .

Smart English - It is his jingoism.

25. Simple English - Bread smells stale.

Smart English - Bread smells musty.

26. Simple English - Release your mental stress.

Smart English - Unload your mental bucket.

27. Simple English - She prepares delicious recipes .

Smart English - She prepares lip smacking recipes .

28. Simple English - You must share your gifts with your friends.

Smart English - You must share your goodies with your friends.

29. Simple English - Ruchika was taking rest in the afternoon in the garden.

Smart English - Ruchika was taking a siesta in the garden.

 Or

After lunch and a siesta, Ruchika's mother made coffee.

30. Simple English - The bad- tempered gardener chased the children.

Smart English - The grouchy gardener chased the children.

31. Simple English - He is angry.

Smart English - He is testy.

32. Simple English - The angry principal gave harsh punishment to the students.

Smart English - The sullen Principal gave harsh punishment to his students.

33. Simple English - The child was angry.

Smart English - The child was grumpy.

34. Simple English - The youth were angry as they were not allowed to swim.

Smart English - The youth were peevish as they were not allowed to swim.

35. Simple English - It is difficult to read his handwriting.

Smart English - His handwriting is illegible.

36. Simple English - It is difficult to read.

Smart English - It is difficult to decipher.

37. Simple English - This is a good idea talked over by China.

Smart English - This is a good idea mooted by China.

38. Simple English - I have a troublesome relative.

Smart English - I have a pesky relative.

39. Simple English - Hope you will agree to my request.

Smart English - Hope you will accede to my request.

40. Simple English - Stick to the rules and regulations of the school.

Smart English - Adhere to the rules and regulations of the school.

41. Simple English - Farewell was given to the teacher.

Smart English - Adieu was given to the teacher.

42. Simple English - Nowadays people are busy in gathering wealth.

Smart English - Nowadays people are busy in amassing wealth.

43. Simple English - Chika said she would make the bill more better.

Smart English - Chika said she would amend the bill.

44. Simple English - There will be enough food and drinks at the party.

Smart English - There will be ample food and drinks at the party.

45. Simple English - Rohan began to hate his favourite sport.

Smart English - Rohan began to abhor his favourite sport.

46. Simple English - When I saw light in the house after midnight, I knew something was wrong .

Smart English - When I saw light in the house after midnight I knew something was amiss.

47. Simple English - His novel won a high praise from literary committee.

Smart English - His novel won great acclaim from literary committee.

48. Simple English - His friends were very considerate and helpful.

Smart English - His friends were very considerate and accommodating.

49. Simple English - His mother cautioned him not to ruin his appetite by eating desert before dinner.

Smart English - His mother admonished him not to ruin his appetite by eating dessert before dinner.

50. Simple English - The hall was decorated with festoons.

Smart English - The hall was adorned with festoons.

Simple English to Smart English

Lesson -9

1. Simple English - He keep himself away from other's company.

Smart English - He keeps himself aloof.

2. Simple English - He is very friendly.

Smart English - He is very amiable.

3. Simple English - I just stopped at everything else he said.

Smart English - I just balked at everything else he said.

4. Simple English - Archita was so shy. she didn't answer my question.

Smart English - Archita was so bashful . She didn't answer my question.

5. Simple English - Public servants should be praised for their good and kind act.

Smart English - Public servants should be commended for their benevolent acts.

6. Simple English - The leaders were too much energetic during the rally.

Smart English - The leaders were incredibly boisterous during rally.

7. Simple English - Sumit's frankness was a shock to all who heard his speech .

Smart English - Sumit's candor was a shock to all who heard his speech .

8. Simple English - He is very cunning person.

Smart English - He is canny person.

9. Simple English - When announcement was made, utter disorder broke out in the hall.

Smart English - When announcement was made utter chaos broke out in the hall.

10. Simple English - Rules should be written in brief.

Smart English - Rules should be written in concise way.

11. Simple English - My friends pleasant smile depicted his kind heart.

Smart English - My friends congenial smile bespoke his

---

kind heart.

12. Simple English - There is lack of furniture in Government schools.

Smart English - There is dearth of furniture in Government schools.

13. Simple English - The coach refused to let down the status of his players.

Smart English - The coach refused to demean his players.

14. Simple English - Don't discourage him.

Smart English - Don't deter him.

15. Simple English - Intolerant people try to scorn all those who disagree with them.

Smart English - Intolerant people try to disdain all those who disagree with them.

16. Simple English - His activity is doubtful.

Smart English - His activity is dubious.

17. Simple English - Public was spellbound to see the wonderful performance of the student.

Smart English - Public was enthralled to see the wonderful performance of the students.

18. Simple English - My mother is the embodiment of courage.

Smart English - My mother is the epitome of courage.

19. Simple English - Always shun(leave) the wrong.
Smart English - Always eschew the wrong.

20. Simple English - We should never criticize anyone excessively.
Smart English - We should never criticize anyone exorbitantly.

21. Simple English - My sports teacher praised the players.
Smart English - My sports teacher extolled the players.

22. Simple English - My friend rejoiced after his wonderful result.
Smart English - My friend exulted after his wonderful result.

23. Simple English - Rohan is false bunch of lies.
Smart English - Rohan is a fallacious bunch of lies.

24. Simple English - It is truly difficult to fully understand.
Smart English - It is truly difficult to fathom.

25. Simple English - My boss showed great patience in a difficult situation.
Smart English - My boss showed great forbearance in a

difficult situation.

26. Simple English - He is unlucky.
Smart English - He is hapless.

27. Simple English - The kid was disdainful (scornful).
Smart English - The kid was haughty.

28. Simple English - My madam was speechless.
Smart English - My madam was ineffable.

29. Simple English - My best friend has inborn talent to paint.
Smart English - My friend is born with innate talent to paint.

30 Simple English - I have too much thirst for knowledge .
Smart English - I have insatiable thirst for knowledge.

31. Simple English - After the incredible performance, the Principal cheerfully praised the children.
Smart English - After the incredible performance, the Principal cheerfully gave kudos to the children.

32. Simple English - Remove the darkness from your mind.
Smart English - Dispel the darkness from your mind.

---

33. Simple English - Boys are disobeying the rule to not cross speed limit.

Smart English - Boys are flouting the speed limit.

34. Simple English - I have many reasons for not going.

Smart English - I have manifold reasons for not going.

35. Simple English - Having to clean a dirty place alone is burdensome work to do .

Smart English - Having to clean a dirty place alone is an onerous chore to do.

36. Simple English - Trying to soothe (calm) both sides in debate, the news anchor proposed many other reasons for the given topic.

Smart English - Trying to pacify both sides in debate the news anchor proposed many reasons for the given topic.

37. Simple English - The food is too tasty.

Smart English - The food is palatable.

38. Simple English - There is no single remedy for all illness .

Smart English - There is no panacea for all illness.

39. Simple English - Using computer for primary teaching tool is certainly an example that is perfect model shift for our teacher.

Smart English - Using computer for primary teaching too

is certainly a paradigm shift for our teachers.

40. Simple English - The greatest issue here is how to solve this problem.

Smart English - The paramount issue here is how to solve this problem.

41. Simple English - Even the PM showed his sympathy for the stricken family.

Smart English - Even the PM showed pathos for the stricken family.

42. Simple English - During flood small quantity of food was available.

Smart English - During flood there was paucity of available food.

43. Simple English - Children were confused.

Smart English - Children were perplexed.

44. Simple English - He was at the highest point of his success.

Smart English - He was at the pinnacle of his success.

45. Simple English - Various activities were performed on the stage.

Smart English - Plethora of activities were performed on the stage.

---

46. Simple English - Her mother gives him toys to calm him.

Smart English - Her mother gives him toys to appease him.

47. Simple English - His greed led him to gather excess wealth.

Smart English - His avarice led him to amass wealth.

48. Simple English - She remained quiet in the dance party.

Smart English - She remained demure in dance party.

49. Simple English - He gave an expressive speech on independence day.

Smart English - He gave an eloquent speech on Independence Day .

50. Simple English - I am very sensitive for my pet when it is upset.

Smart English - I feel empathy for my pet when it is upset.

Simple English to Smart English

Lesson -10

1. Simple English - My Principal praised me for my good performance in sports.

Smart English - My Principal extolled me for my good performance.

2. Simple English - I am surprised (astonished) when I see some unique thing.

Smart English - I am flabbergasted when I see some unique thing.

3. Simple English - I won't give up my principles.

Smart English - I won't forsake my Principles.

4. Simple English - Amit's scornful proud will backfire on him someday.

Smart English - Amit's haughty nature will backfire on him someday.

5. Simple English - If your grades were as exemplary as your elder brother, then you too would receive a smart phone.

Smart English - If your grades were as impeccable as your elder brother, then you too would receive a smart Phone.

6. Simple English - My children are lazy, they can't even polish their shoes.

Smart English - My children are indolent, they can't even polish their shoes.

7. Simple English - The ill repute of his crime will not lessen as time passes by.

Smart English - The infamy of his crime will not lessen as time passes by.

8. Simple English - I did not mean to prevent you from going out.

Smart English - I did not mean to inhibit you from going out.

9. Simple English - The crowd was extremely happy when they saw their favourite star on the stage.

Smart English - The crowd was jubilant when they saw their favourite star on the stage.

10. Simple English - Mr Das is an independent person and always does things in his own way.

Smart English - Mr Das is real maverick person and always does things in his own way.

11. Simple English - Richa's gloomy nature made her very unpleasant to talk to.

Smart English - Richa's morose nature made her very unpleasant to talk to.

12. Simple English - Our city Lucknow presented us with many possibility of fun on independence day

Smart English - Our city Lucknow presented us with myriad possibility of fun on independence day.

13. Simple English - Don't make hasty decision, as haste makes waste.

Smart English - Don't make rash decision, as haste makes waste.

14. Simple English - My mother is too weak.

Smart English - My mother is feeble.

15. Simple English - His hard work was of no use.

Smart English - His hard work was of no avail.

16. Simple English - The problem will remain the same.

Smart English - The problem will persist.

17. Simple English - Please tell it again.

Smart English - Pardon me.

18. Simple English - Sorry for my mistake.

Smart English - I apologize for my mistake.

19. Simple English - It is really too hot.
Smart English - It is really scorcher.

20. Simple English - We are in the hottest days of summer.
Smart English - We are in the dog days of summer.

21. Simple English - It is easy.
Smart English - It is a child's play
 Or
It is a piece of cake.
 Or
It is as easy as pie.

22. Simple English - I didn't have time to prepare for the talk. So I spoke without preparation.
Smart English - I didn't have time to prepare for the talk. So, I winged it.

23. Simple English - My friend Ratna is very intelligent and full of energy.
Smart English - My friend Ratna is a bright spark.

24. Simple English - I usually spend time with old people.
Smart English - I usually hang with the old people.

25. Simple English - I wrote down the notes immediately .

Smart English - I jot down the notes immediately.

26. Simple English - Really I had to bear many things which I don't like.

Smart English - Really I had to grin and bear many things Which I don't like.

27. Simple English - Sometimes people have to be fair even to a person whom they don't like.

Smart English - Sometime people have to give the devil his due.

28. Simple English - You have dressed up handsomely and colourfully.

Smart English - You have dressed up like a peacock.

29. Simple English - Get rid of that old computer.

Smart English - Cast aside that old computer.

30. Simple English - I am tired.

Smart English - I am worn out.

31. Simple English - Go ahead, I support you.

Smart English - Go ahead. You have my backing.

32. Simple English - Your elder brother will go crazy, if you damage his bike .

Smart English - Your elder brother will go bananas if you damage his bike.

33. Simple English - My father is above 70, but still he is healthy and active.

Smart English - My father is above 70, but he is still full of beans.

34. Simple English - You can't fool Ishita. She can't be easily deceived.

Smart English - You can't fool Ishita, She is a sharp cookie.

35. Simple English - My job is interesting but salary is low.

Smart English - My job is interesting but I am paid peanuts.

36. Simple English - Our PM will have to deal with a few sensitive and controversial matter.

Smart English - Our PM will have to deal with a few hot potatoes.

37. Simple English - Aamir khan has been enjoying a period of success since the success of his last film.

Smart English - Aamir khan has been riding hide since the success of his last film.

38. Simple English - Swami Ramdev's products are very successful . He is on top of success.

Smart English - Swami Ramdev's products are very successful. He is on the crest of wave right now.

39. Simple English - If you obtain a high score in English test, you can go for movie.

Smart English - If you ace your English test, you can go for movie.

40. Smart English - He is not intelligent.

Smart English - He is not the sharpest knife in the drawer.

41. Simple English - He is not intelligent.

Smart English - He can't put two and two together.

Or

He is a dumb post .

42. Simple English - He is very intelligent.

Smart English - He is really on the ball.

Or

He is a bright spark.

or

He has got her head screwed on right .

Or

He is quick off the mark.

Or

He is sharp cookie.

Or

He is a walking encyclopedia.

43. Simple English - He is very thin.

Smart English - He is bag of bones.

44. Simple English - My Principal spoke angrily to me for arriving late.

Smart English - My Principal bit my head off for arriving late.

45. Simple English - Snigdha looked very unhappy and discouraged.

Smart English - Snigdha looked bit down in the mouth today.

46. Simple English - The shopkeeper was very irritating and annoying.

Smart English - The shopkeeper was a real pain in the neck.

47. Simple English - The thief promised to behave well when he was arrested.

Smart English - The thief promised to keep his nose clean when he was arrested.

48. Simple English - She was extremely surprised when she heard the noise.

Smart English - She nearly jumped out of her skin when she heard the noise.

49. Simple English - My friend decided to be silent rather than argue.

Smart English - My friend bit her tongue rather than

argue.

50. Simple English - I am hungry.
Smart English - I am famished.
Or
My tummy is talking.
Or
I am starving.

Simple English to Smart English

Lesson -11

1. Simple English - I am in love.

Smart English - i) I am smitten.

ii) I am head over heels.

iii) I am besotted.

iv) I am love sick.

v) I am madly in love.

2. Simple English - I am very happy.

Smart English - i) I am elated.

ii) I am overjoyed.

iii) I am on cloud nine.

iv) I am over the moon.

v) I am on top of the world.

vi) I am delighted.

3. Simple English - Do something.

Smart English - i) Go for it! Why not.

ii) You only live once.

iii) What are you waiting for?

iv) It is worth shot.

4. Simple English - It is very cheap.

Smart English - i) It is a bargain.

ii) It is a steal.

iii) It is as cheap as chips!

iv) It is value for money.

5. Simple English - It is very easy!

Smart English - It is a piece of cake.

6. Simple English - He is calm and in control.

Smart English - He is as cool as a cucumber.

7. Simple English - Don't encourage her.

Smart English - Don't egg her on !

8. Simple English - You will have to admit to your mistake.

Smart English - You will have to eat humble pie.

9. Simple English - He is very clever.

Smart English - He is a smart cookie.

10. Simple English - Really it happened unexpectedly.

Smart English - Really it is a stroke of luck.

11. Simple English - It is a good opportunity.

Smart English - It is luck break.

12. Simple English - I don't want more food.

Smart English - i) I am full.

ii) I had plenty.

iii) I had enough.

Iv) I am stuffed.

13. Simple English - I am very tired.

Smart English - i) I am knackered.

ii) I am exhausted.

iii) I am worn out.

iv) I am on last legs.

v) I am spent.

14. Simple English - I will spend lavishly.

Smart English - i) I will go on a shopping spree.

ii) I will go on a shopping binge.

iii) I will spend money like water.

iv) I will push the boat out.

v) I will splash out.

15. Simple English - I want to stay in bed longer than

usual.

Smart English - i) I will have a lie –in.

ii) I am having a duvet day.

iii) I am having a lazy morning.

16. Simple English - Calm down.

Smart English - i) Steady on!

ii) Chill out.

iii) Control yourself.

iv) Go easy.

17. Simple English - It is too cold.

Smart English - i) It is nippy.

ii) It is chilly.

ii) It is brass monkey out there.

iii) It is bitterly cold.

iv) It is frosty.

18. Simple English - It is great view.

Smart English - i) It is awe –inspiring.

ii) It takes my breath away.

iii) It is jaw - dropping.

iv) It is out of this world.

v) It is like a picture postcard.

19. Simple English - It was a bad day.

Smart English - It was a bad hair day.

20. Simple English - Relax and enjoy yourself.

Smart English - Let your hair down.

21. Simple English - Don't annoy someone, by staying around all the time.

Smart English - Don't get in one's hair.

22. Simple English - Stop being angry or upset.

Smart English - Keep your hair on!

23. Simple English - I don't know.

Smart English - i) I have no idea.

 ii) I have not the faintest idea.

 iii) I haven't the foggiest idea.

24. Simple English - I was studying overnight.

Smart English - i) I am burning the midnight oil.

 ii) I will have to pull all – nighter.

 iii) I am working till the small hour.

 iii) I am working the graveyard shift.

25. Simple English - You are talented.

Smart English - i) You are natural.

 ii) You have got a gift for it.

 iii) You are cut out for it.

 iv) You were born to do it.

---

26. Simple English - It is tasty.
Smart English - i)It is yummy!
ii) It is delish!
iii) It is delicious.
iv) It is luscious.

27. Simple English - Wait!
Smart English - i) Hold a minute!
ii) Hang a minute.
iii) Bear with me.
iv) Let me think about it.
v) No need to hurry.

28. Simple English - Hurry up!
Smart English - i) Jump to it.
ii) Put your skates on.
iii) Make it snappy.
iv) Move it.
v) Shake a leg.
vi) Snap to it.

29. Simple English - Produce new idea.
Smart English - Think up!

30. Simple English - Find some solution.
Smart English - Come up with some solution.

31. Simple English - Start something.
Smart English - Start over.

32. Simple English - Find the answer.
Smart English - Figure out.

33. Simple English - Continue to do it, though it is difficult.
Smart English - Stick to it, though it is difficult.

34. Simple English - Continue to do your work.
Smart English - Keep at your work.

35. Simple English - He found out a way to save each money.
Smart English - He figured out a way to save each money.

36. Simple English - I won the highest award at school. I got the result of my hard work.
Smart English - I won the highest award at school. My hard work paid off.

37. Simple English - He withdrew from a commitment.
Smart English - He backed out from a commitment.

38. Simple English - It requires a costly maintenance and difficult to dispose it.
Smart English - It is a white elephant.

39. Simple English - He has established himself securely in the position of the manager.

Smart English - He has dug himself in the position of the manager.

40. Simple English - He found out the real facts.

Smart English - He dug out the real facts.

41. Simple English - We should try to understand the true worth of hard work.

Smart English - We should try to understand the dignity of labour.

42. Simple English - It doesn't suit you to grant a favour for monetary benefit.

Smart English - It is beneath your dignity to grant a favour for monetary benefit.

43. Simple English - I refused to accept bribe.

Smart English - I stood up on my dignity and refused to accept hush money.

44. Simple English - I raised my voice when I was not treated properly.

Smart English - I stood up on my dignity when I was not treated properly at the function.

45. Simple English - We should never play a mean trick on anybody.

Smart English - We should never play a dirty trick on anybody.

46. Simple English - He lectured upon the necessity of being economical in daily life.

Smart English - He discoursed upon the necessity of being economical.

47. Simple English - Such improper behaviour will make you unpopular with your friend.

Smart English - Such improper behaviour will discredit you with your friends.

48. Simple English - We must be very careful in the choices of books.

Smart English - You must show good discretion in the choices of books.

49. Simple English - Lala Lajpat Rai died for his country.

Smart English - Lala Lajpat Rai died for the sake of his country.

50. Simple English - Government employees doesn't stay at one place because of transfer.

Smart English - Government employees are birds of passage as their posts are transferable.

Simple English to Smart English
Lesson -12

1. Simple English - Principal of our school makes the student obey the rules.

Smart English - Principal of our school leads the children by the nose.

2. Simple English - His fame spread at all places.

Smart English - His fame spread far and wide.

3. Simple English - His dealings are based on justice.

Smart English - His dealings are fair and square.

4. Simple English - I gave him extra discount above the normal discount

Smart English - I gave him extra discount over and above the normal discount.

5. Simple English - During elections many common men became winners.

Smart English - During election many dark horses emerged as winners.

6. Simple English - He is totally merged in debt.

Smart English - He is neck deep in debt.

7. Simple English - Everybody is questioning about high inflation.

Smart English - High inflation is a burning question these days.

8. Simple English - The old man has seen success and failures many times.

Smart English - The old man has seen many ups and downs.

9. Simple English - A common people cannot stand against the powerful people.

Smart English - A common people cannot stand against the high and mighty.

10. Simple English - Though he had done something wrong he told a lie to save himself from punishment.

Smart English - Though he had done something wrong he told a lie to save his skin.

11. Simple English - Recently I have had a lot of Maths homework. This weekend any how I have to complete my

English Work.

Smart English - Recently I have had a lot of Maths homework. This weekend I need to catch up on my English work.

12. Simple English - On my way home from work, I met Renu at her home.

Smart English - On my way home from my work, I dropped in on Renu at her house.

13. Simple English - Can you send this mail at the post office?

Smart English - Can you drop this mail off at the post office?

14. Simple English - Mohit left school when he was 13 years old.

Smart English - Mohit dropped out of school when he was 13 years old.

15. Simple English - The committee rejected the new salary proposal.

Smart English - The committee voted down the new salary proposal.

16. Simple English - She gave up her official job.

Smart English - She stand down her official job.

17. Simple English - She was accepted and chosen for office by just a few votes.

Smart English - She got in by just few votes.

18. Simple English - Rohit Suggested a new idea.

Smart English - Rohit came up with a new idea.

19. Simple English - His business venture failed, So he started it again.

Smart English - His business venture failed, so started over again.

20. Simple English - Find out the answer.

Smart English - Figure out the solution.

21. Simple English - He was behaving in a silly and noisy way in the kitchen and broke my favourite bowl.

Smart English - He was horsing round in the kitchen and broke my favourite bowl.

22. Simple English - When I asked my Principal to raise my salary she refused me.

Smart English - When I asked my Principal to raise my salary, she brushed me off.

23. Simple English - I was late for school this morning, so I ate my breakfast quickly.

Smart English - I was late for school this morning, so I wolfed down my breakfast.

24. Simple English - I am just relaxing in front of the TV.

Smart English - I am just chilling in front of the TV.

or

I am exhausted today so I 'm just going to chill out tonight.

25. Simple English - Wait ! I will be back in a minute.

Smart English - Hang on ! I'll be back in a minute.

26. Simple English - He is a friend of mine from school.

Smart English - He is a buddy of mine from school.

27. Simple English - They just met me, but they are talking and laughing together like old friends.

Smart English - They just met me, but they are talking and laughing together like old chums.

28. Simple English - Reeta and sunita met in high school and have been friends for ten years.

Smart English - Reeta and Sunita met in high school and have been pals for ten years.

29. Simple English - My uncle speaks fondly of his friends from his youth.

Smart English - My uncle speaks fondly of his comrades from his youth.

30. Simple English - Seema is my most trusted friend.

Smart English - Seema is my most trusted confidant.

---

31. Simple English - I love to go to the gym with my friend.

Smart English - I love to go to the gym with my bestie.

32. Simple English - Sumit didn't want to jump, but his friends kept encouraging him.

Smart English - Sumit didn't want to jump, but his friends kept egging him.

33. Simple English - This cake is delicious . I want to eat another piece.

Smart English - This cake is scrumptious. I want to eat another piece.

34. Simple English - Your dessert looks delicious.

Smart English - Your dessert looks appetizing.

35. Simple English - Your food is delicious.

Smart English - Your food is mouth –watering.

36. Simple English - That ice –cream store makes delicious ice –creams.

Smart English - That ice cream store makes yummy ice-creams.

37. Simple English - His stories are boring.

Smart English - His stories are dull.

38. Simple English - This is a boring work.

Smart English - This is a mind- numbing work.

39. Simple English - This is a boring homework assignment.

Smart English - This is a tedious homework assignment.

40. Simple English - He tells old jokes.

Smart English - He tells stale jokes.

41. Simple English - Her story was so interesting that I forgot time.

Smart English - Her story was so engrossing that I lost track of time.

42. Simple English - She told an interesting story.

Smart English - She told an enthralling story.

43. Simple English - His speech was interesting.

Smart English - His speech was captivating.

44. Simple English - Mr. Ashutosh is an interesting man.

Smart English - Mr Ashutosh is an intriguing man.

45. Simple English - Good manners stimulates positive interaction.

Smart English - Good manners fosters positive interaction.

Simple English to Smart English - Sarita Singh

46. Simple English - Bahubali movie is interesting.

Smart English - Bahubali movie is riveting.

47. Simple English - I will take chocolate ice cream.

Smart English - I will go for chocolate ice cream.

48. Simple English - You leave him to me. I will persuade him.

Smart English - You leave him to me. I will work on him.

49. Simple English - I will not dismay him. I will work and make him proud of me.

Smart English - I will work and make her proud of me.I will not let him down.

50. Simple English - I hate the way she makes me feel insulted.

Smart English - I hate the way she puts me down.

Simple English to Smart English

Lesson -13

1. Simple English - He was removed from the company.

Smart English - He was kicked out of the company.

2. Simple English - You have made a mistake, just erase and start again.

Smart English - You have made a mistake, just erase and start over.

3. Simple English - I am suffering from cold.

Smart English - I am coming down with cold. I keep sneezing and have a runny nose.

4. Simple English - She recovered from flu. She is feeling fine now.

Smart English - She got over the flu. She is feeling fine now.

5. Simple English - I laughed in class because Astha told the funniest joke.

Smart English - I cracked up in class because Astha told the funniest joke.

6. Simple English - You have been working hard . You should reward yourself and enjoy on Sunday.

Smart English - You have been working hard. You should reward yourself and goof off on Sunday.

7. Simple English - I was talking to my incharge when Jyoti interrupted.

Smart English - I was talking to my in charge, then Jyoti butted in.

8. Simple English - She is a brave traveller.
Smart English - She is a dauntless traveller.

9. Simple English - The team showed a brave effort.
Smart English - The team showed a gallant effort.

10. Simple English - It is so strange.
Smart English - It is so weird.

11. Simple English - No excuses.
Smart English - No ifs or buts.

12. Simple English - Hope your health is good.

Smart English - Hope you are in pink of your health.

13. Simple English - He ate too much.
Smart English - He ate like a horse.

14. Simple English - He ignored my advice.
Smart English - He turned a deaf ear to my advice.

15. Simple English - The news is hidden from the public.
Smart English - The news is under wraps.

16. Simple English - He has forgotten what he was saying or thinking about.
Smart English - He lost his train of thoughts.

17. Simple English - He worked smoothly and regularly.
Smart English - He worked like clockwork.

.

18. Simple English - He is easily targeted.
Smart English - He is a sitting duck.

19. Simple English - Come on ! Get to the point.
Smart English - Come on, cut to chase.

20. Simple English - He is almost out of patience.
Smart English - He is at the end of his rope.

21. Simple English - I will get it through by any means, fair or unfair.

Smart English - I will get it done by hook or crook.

22. Simple English - Renu looked totally confused.

Smart English - Renu seemed lost in the woods.

23. Simple English - His mood turned bad when he saw her.

Smart English - His mood darkened on seeing her.

24. Simple English - The crowd became violent.

Smart English - The crowd went on rampage.

25. Simple English - Don't worry, he is a good subordinate and will follow your order.

Smart English - Don't worry, he will work under your thumb.

26. Simple English - It will be a surprise for you.

Smart English - It will be an eye opener for you.

27. Simple English - It simply meant to deceive you.

Smart English - I think it is just a smoke screen.

28. Simple English - We are not in an advantageous position on this job.

Smart English - On this job we are not exactly on home

---

ground.

29. Simple English - Mahesh hasn't taken final decision and is still checking the advantages and disadvantages .

Smart English - Mahesh is still testing the water.

30. Simple English - Krishna could have changed things for the better.

Smart English - Krishna could have turned it around.

31. Simple English - Ramu began laughing.

Smart English - Ramu broke into laughter.

32. Simple English - Ruchika impressed the child.

Smart English - Ruchika made a mark on the little mind.

33. Simple English - Anil kumar hypnotised the audience.

Smart English - Atul kumar cast magic on the crowd.

34. Simple English - Be ready to fight it out .

Smart English - Be ready to go on the mat.

35. Simple English - All my projects have failed.

Smart English - All my projects have run into the ground.

36. Simple English - In trying to save petty amounts, do not end up losing large sums.

Smart English - Don't be penny wise and pound foolish.

37. Simple English - Narendra doesn't show any emotions.

Smart English - Narendra is an ice berg.

38.Simple Engish - Naresh came up with a money spinning idea.

Smart English - Naresh came up with pure gold.

39. Simple English - It has been a secret affair from beginning.

Smart English - It's been a hush –hush affair from the beginning.

40. Simple English - Please sit down here.

Smart English - Please park yourself here.

41. Simple English - First drink some water.

Smart English - First quench your thirst.

42. Simple English - Let's begin work.

Smart English - Let's set the ball rolling.

43. Simple English - The new car is expensive.

Smart English - The new car cost us an arm and a leg.

44. Simple English - He became very thin after exams

Smart English - He was a bag of bones after the exams.

45. Simple English - I have forgotten to bring my lunch. I have bad memory.

Smart English - I have forgotten to bring my lunch, I have got a brain like a sieve.

46. Simple English - He is flattering the boss, he wants a job.

Smart English - He is buttering the boss, he wants a job.

47. Simple English - My mother is growing old.

Smart English - My mother is getting on in years.

48. Simple English - The view of hilly area was beautiful.

Smart English - The view of hilly area was stunning.

49. Simple English - You are looking beautiful.

Smart English - You are looking gorgeous.

50. Simple English - No need to be afraid, Principal is extremely gentle and calm.

Smart English - No need to be afraid, Principal is as gentle as a lamb.

Simple English to smart English
Lesson - 14

1.Simple English - Eat every bite of food in the remembrance of God.

Smart English - Eat every morsel in the remembrance of God.

2. Simple English - There is no improper (dubious, doubtful) things involved.

Smart English - There is no hanky –panky involved.

3. Simple English - It is doubtful.

Smart English - It is dubious.

4. Simple English - Amrit put your idea into action.

Smart English - Amrit get the show on the road.

5. Simple English - Come on! Do something new for the

company. We no longer want obsolete things.

Smart English - Come on! Do something new for the company. We no longer want the dead wood.

6. Simple English - Two of the junior teachers are trying to replace the senior teacher.

Smart English - Two of the junior teachers are waiting in wings to replace the senior teacher.

7. Simple English - My most respected teacher is number one.

Smart English - My most revered teacher is numero uno.

8. Simple English - Don't do anything in hurry, as it will become waste.

Smart English- Don't do anything in hasty manner, as haste makes waste.

9. Simple English - Tourists are being troubled by the unruly taxi drivers.

Smart English - Tourists are being harassed by the unruly taxi drivers.

10 Simple English - I got fully soaked in rain.

Smart English - I got fully drenched in rain.

11. Simple English - It was by chance that I met with my favourite actor.

Smart English - It was a coincidence that I met my

favourite actor.

12. Simple English - I desire to become a doctor.
Smart English - I yearn to become a doctor.

13. Simple English - She bears up the odd situation boldly.
Smart English-She copes up the odd situation boldly.

14.Simple English - Let us go for leisurely walk.
Smart English - Let us stroll.

15. Simple English - Eat fresh food in the morning, not the leftover of night .
Smart English - Eat fresh food, not the stale food.

16. Simple English - It is old news.
Smart English- It is a stale news.

17. Simple English - He is healthy.
Smart English - He is hale and hearty.

18. Simple English- Don't feel jealous of your friend.
Smart English - Don't envy your friend.

19. Simple English - Don't speak in low voice.
Smart English - Don't murmur.

---

20. Simple English - It was quite surprising.
Smart English - It was astounding.

21. Simple English - His whole behaviour seems to change.
Smart English - His whole demeanour seems to change.

22. Simple English - He jumped with happiness.
Smart English - He hopped with happiness.

23. Simple English- I regret on my past.
Smart English- I lament on my past.

24. Simple English - The farmer was in deep sadness after the death of his wife.
Smart English - The farmer was in grief after the death of his wife.

25. Simple English - You can make or end your career.
Smart English - You can make or mar your career.

26. Simple English-We should increase our power or tolerance to do some difficult task.
Smart English - We should increase stamina or endurance to do some difficult task.

27. Simple English - National flag was hoisted on Independence Day.

Smart English - National flag was unfurled on Independence Day.

28. Simple English - I expected a good result but had never thought that I would get such a good success.

Smart English - I expected a good result but had never thought that I would fare so well.

29. Simple English - He reads too much.

Smart English - He is a book worm.

30. Simple English - I was too happy.

Smart English - I was overwhelmed.

31. Simple English - Foul smell is coming from toilet.

Smart English - Toilet is stinking.

32. Simple English - Bad language is written on the wall.

Smart English - Foul language is written on the wall.

Or

Filthy language is written on the wall.

33. Simple English - The condition of poor people is very bad in our country.

Smart English - The condition of poor people is pathetic in our country.

34. Simple English - Vendors cover the footpath which is

used by foot walkers.

Smart English - Vendors cover the footpath which is used by pedestrians.

35. Simple English - Surroundings of many schools are very dirty.

Smart English - Surroundings of many schools are unkempt.

36. Simple English - Miseries of river Ganga must be taken care of.

Smart English - Woes of river Ganga must be taken care of.

37. Simple English - The ownerless animals in the city have increased in number recently.

Smart English - The stray animals in the city have increased in number recently.

38. Simple English - The animals prove obstruction in the smooth flow of traffic.

Smart English - The animals prove hurdles in the smooth flow of traffic.

39. Simple English - Unfortunately the forest area of our country is finishing.

Smart English - Unfortunately the forest area of our country is depleting.

40. Simple English - I will rejoin my duty on Monday.

Smart English - I will resume my duty on Monday.

41. Simple English - The electricity is highly irregular and uncertain.

Smart English - The Electricity is highly erratic and uncertain.

42. Simple English - There are many great and beautiful works of art in India.

Smart English - There are many great and exquisite works of art in India.

43. Simple English - Don't interfere in my personal matters.

Smart English - Don't intervene in my personal matters.

44. Simple English - A bad health lowers a man's self-regard.

Smart English - A bad health lowers a man's self–esteem.

45. Simple English - Take some corrective measure in this regard.

Smart English - Take some remedial measure in this regard.

46. Simple English- Be careful of such fake institutions.

Smart English - Be wary of such fake institutions.

47. Simple English-Such institutions cheat the people in

the name of education.

Smart English- Such institutions dupe the people in the name of education.

48. Simple English - My friend is quite thin.

Smart English - My friend is quite sleek.

49. Simple English - It is hard to oppose.

Smart English - It is hard to resist.

50. Simple English - Come to Lucknow, You will be taken to all the beautiful sights of Lucknow.

Smart English - Come to Lucknow, You will be taken to all the endearing sights of Lucknow.

Simple English to smart English

Lesson -15

1. Simple English - You will be amazed with the attractive sounds of beaches.

Smart English - You will be amazed with the enchanting sounds of beaches.

2. Simple English- There are blind followers of religion who do not understand religion at all.

Smart English - There are bigots of religion who do not understand religion at all.

3. Simple English - The annual function is always celebrated with great enthusiasm.

Smart English- The annual function is celebrated with gusto.

4. Simple English - My teacher didn't come.

Smart English - My teacher didn't turn up.

5. Simple English - A healthy environment helps to turn away negativity.

Smart English - A healthy environment helps to avert negativity.

6. Simple English - She has got very beautiful sense.

Smart English - She has got aesthetic sense.

7. Simple English- Musicians of the world are held in high respect.

Smart English - Musicians of the world are held in high esteem.

8. Simple English- The importance of music is really great.

Smart English - The importance of music is immense.

9. Simple English - Bonded labourers work on very low wage.

Smart English - Bonded labourers work on meagre wage.

10. Simple English - This is a life taking disease.

Smart English - This is a fatal disease.

11. Simple English - Gathering arms is a threat to world peace.

Smart English - Amassing arms is a threat to world peace.

12. Simple English - We should think about advantage

and disadvantage of the things before doing anything.

Smart English - We should think about pros and cons of the things before doing anything.

13. Simple English - We should not be charmed by TV advertisement.

Smart English - We should not be lured by TV advertisements.

14. Simple English - In the name of health misleading advertisements sell useless things.

Smart English - In the name of health misleading advertisements sell trash.

15. Simple English - Children spend no time on exercise. They always sit and watch TV.

Smart English - Children are becoming couch potatoes.

16. Simple English - Children becomes lazy and listless by sitting and watching TV.

Smart English - Children live a sedentary life by always watching TV.

17. Simple English - Children have a liking for junk food.

Smart English - Children have crush on Junk food.

18. Simple English - We must avoid eating junk food.

Smart English - We must abstain from eating junk food.

---

19. Simple English - Cake is too tasty.

Smart English - Cake is palatable.

20. Simple English - Fast food is dangerous for health.

Smart English - Fast food is hazardous for health.

21. Simple English - It is so dirty.

Smart English - It is shabby.

22. Simple English - Education is the key to all diseases like poverty, health etc.

Smart English - Education is the key to all maladies like poverty, health etc.

23. Simple English - With one voice we should fight against poverty.

Smart English - Unanimously we should fight against poverty.

24. Simple English - He is finding out my secret.

Smart English - He is spying out my secret.

25. Simple English - It is sufficient.

Smart English - It is suffice.

 Or

It is enough.

26. Simple English-Rains are becoming less.

Smart English - Rains are becoming scanty.

27. Simple English - There is a great need to take immediate steps in this regard.

Smart English- There is dire need to take immediate steps in this regard.

28. Simple English - Forest areas are affected by forest fire.

Smart English - Forest areas are prone to forest fire.

29. Simple English - The residence area of Bihar people were under the water.

Smart English - The residence area of Bihar people were submerged in water.

30. Simple English - A bitter anger is prevailing amongst students against the Principal.

Smart English - A bitter resentment is prevailing amongst students against the Principal.

31. Simple English - India has strength and ability to contain an amazing diversity within itself.

Smart English - India has vigour and ability to contain an amazing diversity within itself.

32. Simple English - The destructive people in our society creates disturbance.

Smart English - The hooligans in our society creates disturbance.

Or

The rogues in our society creates disturbance.

33. Simple English - The self- willed girls and boys don't follow the rules of school.

Smart English - The wayward girls and boys don't follow the rules of school.

34. Simple English - The future of boys and girls are at risk.

Smart English - The future of boys and girls are at stake.

35. Simple English - He believes in age old thinking.

Smart English - He is conservative.

36. Simple English - I am grateful to you.

Smart English - I am obliged.

37. Simple English - He is quite innocent.

Smart English - He is unwary.

38. Simple English - He is a treasure of knowledge.

Smart English- He is a reservoir of knowledge.

39. Simple English - It is possible.

Smart English - It is feasible.

40. Simple English - It is impossible.

Smart English - It is not feasible.

41. Simple English - Physical health helps a lot to maintain the human body in order.

Smart English - Physical health helps a lot to maintain the human body in tune.

42. Simple English - Education without moral is a danger for society.

Smart English - Education without moral creates menace in society.

43. Simple English - Today's game of politics is full of great fear.

Smart English- Today's game of politics is horrendous.

44. Simple English - Today we are stuck (twisted with something else) in the web of corruption.

Smart English - Today we are entangled in the web of corruption.

45. Simple English - Let us all come together and work with firm decision.

Smart English - Let us all work resolutely with firm decision.

46. Simple English - She took me in her arms when I met her after a long gap.

Smart English - She hugged me in her arms when I met her after a long gap.

Or

She embraced me in her arms when I met her after a long gap.

47. Simple English - Satisfy your thirst.
Smart English - Quench your thirst.

48. Simple English- He thought over that topic.
Smart English - He mused over that topic.

49. Simple English - That place presented a strange silence.
Smart English - That place presented an eerie silence.

50. Simple English - The door has stopped giving out rough sound.
Smart English - The door has stopped giving a clicking and jarring sound.

Simple English to smart English
Lesson -16

1. Smart English - Don't look into my copy.
Smart English - Don't peep into my copy.

2. Simple English - I had a quick look at my watch.
Smart English - I peeked at my watch.

3. Simple English - It was a terrible accident.
Smart English - It was a ghastly accident.

4. Simple English - Proper reply was given to the students.
Smart English - Befitting reply was given to the students.

5. Simple English - An uncontrolled bus conductor was beating the students.
Smart English - An unruly bus conductor was beating the students.

6. Simple English - Aligarh has earned a defame for communal riots.

Smart English - Aligarh has earned an infamy for communal riots.

7. Simple English - The anti- social elements of our country creates disturbance.

Smart English - The mischief – mongers of our country creates disturbance.

8. Simple English - The fire covered the whole area.

Smart English - The fire engulfed the whole area.

9. Simple English - It haunts our mind.

Smart English - It is mind – boggling.

10. Simple English - Pool of the blood on the road presented a heart tearing tragic sight.

Smart English - Pool of blood on the road presented a heart rendering and tragic sight.

11. Simple English - The bus dashed the car and many died.

Smart English - The bus collided the car and many died.

12. Simple English - The school bus turned upside down.

Smart English - The school bus toppled over.

13. Simple English - Don't ask senseless questions.

Smart English - Don't ask absurd questions.

14. Simple English - It is old fashioned.
Smart English - It is outdated.

15. Simple English - The students were uncontrollable.
Smart English - The students were unbridled.

16. Simple English - The number of vehicles increases manifold to an unmanageable limit.
Smart English - The number of vehicles swells to an unmanageable limit.

17. Simple English - Less number of parking facilities have made the place crowded and compressed.
Smart English - Inadequate parking facilities have made the place cramped and jam-packed.

18. Simple English - Earthquake in Gujarat brought great ruin.
Smart English - Earthquake in Gujarat brought havoc and disaster.

19. Simple English - Don't make your playground dirty.
Smart English - Don't litter your playground.

20. Simple English- Only a quick and adequate aid can save a very serious situation.
Smart English - Only a prompt and adequate aid can save

a very grave situation.

21. Simple English - Other students hated his voice.
Smart English - Other students loathed his voice.

22. Simple English - He is quite stupid.
Smart English - He is quite crass.

23. Simple English - With great joy he sang a song.
Smart English - With great elation he sang a song.

24. Simple English - He sang a sweet song.
Smart English - He sang a melodious song.

25. Simple English - I was completely surprised.
Smart English - I was completely taken aback.
Or
I was dumbstruck.
Or
I was startled.
Or
I was awestruck.

26. Simple English - He listened the speech very carefully and was completely lost.
Smart English - His listened the speech with rapt attention and was completely lost.

27. Simple English - He is lonely and strange person.

Smart English - He is solitary loon person.

28. Simple English - It is very beautiful and fine.

Smart English - It is splendid.

29. Simple English- He was excited and pleased with confidence.

Smart English - He was flashed and pleased with confidence.

30. Simple English - Situation was upside down.

Smart English - Situation was topsy turvy.

31. Simple English - She is a great celebrity.

Smart English - She is a huge sensation.

32. Simple English - My voice has become rough and unclear.

Smart English - My voice has become hoarse.

33. Simple English - In a great anger he broke the cup.

Smart English - In a great rage he broke the cup.

34. Simple English - There is a heavy rain outside.

Smart English - There is a heavy downpour outside.

35. Simple English - My sister is addicted to internet.

Smart English - My Sister is netizen.

36. Simple English - My sister has knowledge of latest technology and gadgets.

Smart English - My sister is tech savvy.

37. Simple English - My friend is very nervous to use modern technology.

Smart English - My friend is technoplegic.

38. Simple English - Rimi tries to gain more respect and fame than other girls.

Smart English - Rimi tries to outshine.

39. Simple English - The two boys did petty(small) job to survive.

Smart English - The two boys did menial job to survive.

40. Simple English - Don't bother what insignificant people say.

Smart English - Don't bother what petty people say.

41. Simple English - She lacks physical beauty.

Smart English - She is homely.

42. Simple English - My sister is fat.

Smart English - My sister is stout.

43. Simple English - Everything in the room was in disorder.

Smart English - Everything in the room was slipshod.

44. Simple English - She is very thin.

Smart English - She is skinny.

45. Simple English - Your handwriting can't be read.

Smart English - Your handwriting is illegible.

46. Simple English - He was wearing worn coat.

Smart English - He was wearing tottered coat.

47. Simple English - Pay attention to what I say.

Smart English - Give heed to what I say.

48. Simple English - We should avoid the pressure of our friends while making decision.

Smart English - We should avoid peer pressure while making decision.

49. Simple English - The students cleaned the ground with the broom.

Simple English - The students wielded the brooms and cleaned the ground.

50. Simple English - The teachers made out a plan.

Smart English - The teachers chalked out a plan.

Words that describe people around you
Lesson 17

Dear Children !

There are certain words which describe people according to their nature. Read and find out the words which describe your friends and the people around you. You will learn how to describe the people.

1. Trustworthy- dependable, reliable

2. Problem solving- who is capable to solve the problem

3. Good orator- who is a good speaker.. speech etc

4. Unassuming- who doesn't show off

5. Authoritative- commanding, masterful

6. Egoistic- proud, full of himself

7. Sympathetic- caring, concerned

8. Dominating- bossy, control over

9. Kind –hearted- loving

10. Thoughtful- absorbed in, meditative

11. Careless- inattentive, negligent

12. Hopeless- despairing, bad, inferior

13. Laborious- hard- working

14. Industrious- hard- working

15. Hard – working who toils hard

16. Diligent- hard- working

17. Irresponsible- careless, reckless

18. Workaholic- who is too much engrossed in his work

19. Accommodative- kind, simple and humble person

20. Sagacious- very intelligent

21. Chatty- who is too talkative, chatty

22. Tiresome- who feels tired

23. Oblivious- who is forgetful

24. Voracious- who feels too hungry

25. Forgetful- who has habit of forgetting

26. Glutton- who feels too hungry

27. Back biter- who talks ill of others their absence

28. Boasting- who is full of himself and praises himself

29. Dowdy- who does his work in a very unorganized way and in messy way

30. Teetotaler- who is not addict of smoking,drinks or any other things

31. Fraud- crook. Who deceives

32. Inhuman - who doesn't love humanity

33. Meticulous person - who does work very carefully

34. Calculating- shrewd, cunning

35. Garrulous- who talks too much

36. Whimsical- who is moody and enjoys his life

37. Accountable- who keeps transparency in his work

38. Honest - who doesn't adopt illegal means for his living

39. Dishonest - who adopts illegal means for his living

40. Dubious person - doubtful

41. Compassionate - kind and loving

42. Benign - open hearted

43. Benevolent - kind

44. Flatterer - who does buttering of his superiors for personal gain

45. Loyal - faithful, reliable

46. Bounteous- open hearted

47. Remissive - who forgives

48. Bountiful - kind hearted

49. Shrewd - cunning

50. Cunning - cunning

51. Clever - crafty

52. Philanthropist- who loves humanity

53. Aggressive- too much angry

54. Affectionate- very loving

55. Ambitious - whose aim is too high

56. Anxious- perplexed,wistful,easeless,vexed

57. Artistic- good in arts

58. Bad- tempered- feels angry on small things

59. Chatterbox- who talks too much, chatty

60. Talkative- who talks too much

61. Big –Hearted- open hearted

62. Boring- not interesting, monotonous

63. Bossy- dominating, controls over

64. Charismatic – attractive

65. Creative- having ability or power to create new things

66. Courageous- plucky, brave

67. Coward - timid- Who is not brave

68. Dependable- reliable

69. Devious- who deceives someone

70. Dim- not intelligent

71. Extrovert- an out going person, sociable person,genial

72. Introvert- a shy, reticent person

73. Bounteous- open- hearted

74. Generous- open- hearted

75. Reluctant- not willing to do anything

76. Short- tempered- angry on petty things

77. Amiable- loving and friendly

78. Amicable- friendly

79. Ruthless- harsh

80. Relentless- harsh

81. Callous- harsh

82. Co operative- who is friendly

83. Cranky- sixty year madness

84. Crazy- mad

85. Gregarious- friendly

86. Impulsive person- who works without thinking

87. Intellectual- intelligent, wise, knowledgeable

88. Joyful- happy by nature

89. Reliable- trustworthy

90. Sociable- who is friendly with everybody

91. Upbeat- optimistic and energetic

92. Plucky- brave, courageous

93. Easy-going- funny

94. Friendly- who mingles with everybody

95. Funny- laughable

96. Grumpy- bad -tempered

97. Lethargic – lazy

98. Loud- out spoken,out going

99. Lucky- whose luck is good

100. Mean - selfish

101. Moody - who works according to his mood, whimcical

102. Nasty- person to whom nobody likes

103. Neat- clean

104. Nervous- who is in tension

105. Polite- humble

106. Popular- famous, reputed,affluent

107. Quiet- calm

108. Rude- bad nature

109. Selfish- who thinks of himself only

110. Serious- sober, earnest, thoughtful in character

111. Shy- bashful

112. Silly- foolish

113. Smart- presentable

114. Stupid- foolish

115. Tidy- neat and clean or spick and span

116. Unlucky- hapless

117. Untidy- not in proper order, mess

118. Vain- (She is really vain . Spends too much time looking mirror) who always thinks about her beauty

119. Wise- intelligent, knowledgeable

120. Adaptable – who adjusts according to situation

121. Adventurous- who takes up dangerous jobs

122. Affable- good natured and friendly

123. Agreeable- Quiet enjoyable and pleasurable

124. Amusing- funny person

125. Bright- intelligent

126. Broad- minded- open- minded, modern

127. Calm- peaceful

128. Careful- who works carefully

129. Charming- who wins heart

130. Communicative- expressive man, frank

131. Conscientious- hard working

132. Considerate- who takes care of others

133. Convivial- genial, affable good humoured, amiable

134. Courteous- good nature

135. Decisive- strong- minded

136. Determined- firm

137. Diplomate- ambassador, on sensitive issue works in tactful way

---

138. Discreete - who talks very carefully

139. Energetic - full of energy and spirit

140. Enthusiastic - full of spirit, energetic

141. Exuberant - cheery, buoyant, vivacious, lively, irrepressible

142. Fair - minded- fair, impartial,egalitarian

143. Faithful - reliable, faithful

144. Fearless - not afraid

145. Forceful - vigorous, dominant, audacious, bold, zealous, self-assured, confident, strong- willed

146. Frank - candid,direct, plain –spoken, straight forward

147. Impartial - who doesn't favour anybody, fair

148. Independent - self- supporting

149. Intuitive- who works according to emotions without fact and proof

150. Modest- Self –effacing,unassuming,humble

151. Submissive- obedient

152. Meek- gentle

153. Docile- compliant, dutiful,passive, submissive, accommodating

154. Naïve- innocent, artless, childlike, simple, unpretentious.

155. Optimistic- who thinks positive

156. Pessimistic- who thinks negative

157. Pioneering- who gives way to new thoughts

158. Philosophical- devoted to the study of fundamental nature of knowledge

159. Placid- even- tempered, tranquil, calm, serene, mild,

easy- going, undisturbed, unexcitable

160. Pro- active- who works immediately, doesn't wait for perfect time

161. Quick- witted- alert, who responds quickly

162. Rational- logical and uses his brain for any work

163. Reserved- who keeps quiet, doesn't express himself much

164. Resourceful- who works intelligently

165. Romantic- who expresses love beautifully

166. Self –Confident- who has confidence on himself

167. Self-Disciplined- who follows discipline

168. Sensible- who uses his brain

169. Sensitive- emotional

170. Straight- forward- Who speaks without any fear on face

171. Tough- harsh

172. Touchy- emotional

173. Versatile- all rounder,multifaceted,multitalented, many-sided

174. Warm – hearted- very friendly

175. Willing- inclined

176. Witty- humorous, funny, chuckle some, comical

177. Discreet- talks in cautious manner

178. Dynamic- Active person, lively positive person

179. Flexible- who adjusts in every situation

180. Babyish- behaves like a kid

182. Classy- superior, elegant, smart, sophisticated

183. Flawed- faulty, erroneous, fallacious

184. Thick–Skinned- Who doesen't bothers about anything

185. Susceptible- Vulnerable,who is easily influenced

186. Well- endowed- wealthy,, well provided with money

187. Arrogant - full of oneself, feeling superior, haughty

188. Humble- meek, docile

189. Crafty- who cleverly gets his work done

190. Scheming- tricky, crafty, sly, artful, cunning,

191. Sly- tricky, crafty, sly, artful, cunning

192. Obedient- Who obeys. Submissive

193. Candid- frank, outspoken, blunt, straightforward honest, plainspoken